Valeri Gorbachev is the author and illustrator of many children's books, both in the United States and in Europe, including *Nicky and the Big Bad Wolves* and *Little Bunny's Sleepless Night*. Mr. Gorbachev emigrated to the United States from the Ukraine in 1991 and now lives with his family in Brooklyn, New York.

Copyright © 2020 by Valeri Gorbachev.
First published in the United States, Great Britain, Canada, Australia, and New Zealand in 2020 by NorthSouth Books, Inc., an imprint of NordSüd Verlag AG, CH-8050 Zürich, Switzerland.

Distributed in the United States by NorthSouth Books, Inc., New York 10016.
Library of Congress Cataloging-in-Publication Data is available.

ISBN: 978-0-7358-4425-4
Printed in Latvia
1 3 5 7 9 · 10 8 6 4 2
www.northsouth.com

There Was a Turkey on the Farm

Valeri Gorbachev

The farm was a busy place.
Everyone was content, except Turkey.

"Why are you always alone and looking so bored?"
asked wise Cow. "Why don't you have any friends?"
   "Because I can't see who I can be friends with on
this farm," said Turkey.

"I would like to be friends with Pig, but she looks very unfriendly to me. . . ."

"I told the ducks that they talk funny, and walk funny too! But they took offense at it. So I can't be friends with them now.

Quack!

Quack!

Quack!

"And I can't imagine someone
with a beard and horns, like Goat,
being my friend.

"And it is impossible to
be friends with Hen because
she only cares about her chicks
all the time."

Cock-a-doodle-doo!

Cock-a-doodle-doo!

Cock-a-doodle-doo!

"And Rooster crows so loudly
in the morning that he gives me a
headache for the rest of the day."

"Oh no!" said wise Cow. "You will never find any friends if you are so choosy."

"I don't think so!" said Turkey.

Then Turkey jumped over the farm fence and
walked toward the pond.

"If I can't find any friends on the farm,
I will try to find them somewhere else!"
she said to herself.

But no matter how much Turkey looked around,
she could not find anyone who could be her friend.

She felt very lonely and bored.

"I'm so beautiful and so nice!" said Turkey, staring at her reflection in the water. "Why can't I find any friends?"

Suddenly Turkey saw someone else's reflection next to hers.
"I'd love to be your friend!" said the reflection.

"And who are you?" asked Turkey.

"I'm Fox, and I want to invite you to the dinner party."

Help!

"Oh no! I am afraid of foxes!" exclaimed Turkey.

"Don't be!" said Fox, and he started pulling Turkey toward the forest.

"Somebody help!" cried Turkey. "Help!"

Turkey yelled so loudly that she was heard even at the farm. "Our Turkey is in trouble!" shouted Rooster from the top of the fence. "She needs our help!"

And everyone rushed to save Turkey.

"Hey, Fox!" they cried. "Let go of our friend!"

"It seems our dinner party will be postponed!" said frightened Fox. "See you next time, Turkey. . . ."

He pushed Turkey away and ran into the forest.
Everyone was so happy to see that poor Turkey was okay.

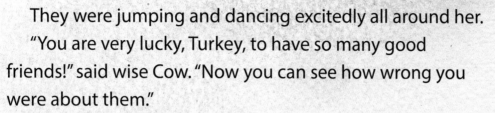

They were jumping and dancing excitedly all around her.

"You are very lucky, Turkey, to have so many good friends!" said wise Cow. "Now you can see how wrong you were about them."

"Yes! I can see it now. They are all wonderful friends!" said Turkey. " And I love them very much!"

And happy Turkey and her friends went back to the farm.